THE DAY MY RUNNY NOSE Ran Away

by **Jason Eaton**

illustrated by **Ethan Long**

DUTTON CHILDREN'S BOOKS • NEW YORK

Dedicated to The Great Bubblegum Caper

Thanks to Tanya McKinnon, Stephanie Owens Lurie, Ian Lendler, Holly Morris, Grant Dawson, and, of course, Montague
J.E.

To my parents, Brenda and Tom, alphabetically, for letting me follow my nose.
E.L.

Text copyright © 2002 by Jason Eaton
Illustrations copyright © 2002 by Ethan Long

CIP Data is available.

Published in the United States 2002 by Dutton Children's Books,
a division of Penguin Putnam Books for Young Readers
345 Hudson Street, New York, New York 10014
www.penguinputnam.com
Designed by Richard Amari
Printed in China
First Edition
10 9 8 7 6 5 4 3 2 1
ISBN 0-525-47013-1

One day a most peculiar thing happened.
When I woke up in the morning, there was a note on my pillow:

Dear Jason,

Last night your mother told you not to wipe your nose on your sleeve. But did you listen? No! You wiped me up and down your lousy sleeve and then blew me on some scratchy paper towels. Well, that was the last straw. You squish me up against windows. You cover the rest of your body in winter but leave me to freeze. You never introduce me to your friends. Why, you've never even taken the time to ask me what my name is! This situation just isn't working for me. I need more. You're a good kid, but I'd prefer we just be friends.

Yours truly,
Montague
(your nose)

P.S. I'll send you a postcard.

This was bad. What would I do without a nose? All the other nose-wearing children would make fun of me. I checked under the bed, just to make sure it hadn't fallen off while I was asleep, but it was no use.

My runny nose had definitely run away.

I wrapped a scarf around my face and made my way downstairs, hoping my mother wouldn't notice anything. No such luck. The moment I sat down at the table, she stopped what she was doing and stared at me. "Jason Carter Eaton," she said in that tone of voice that meant trouble, "where is your nose, young man?"

There was no hiding the truth. "It's gone," I told her.

"You wiped your nose on your sleeve again, didn't you?" she said. "Well, now you've got no nose. I hope you're happy."

Breakfast was apple-cinnamon oatmeal, but I couldn't smell either the apple or the cinnamon. I ate carefully. I didn't want to annoy any other body parts.

The day got worse and worse as it went on. By the time math class started, the whole school knew about my missing nose. I tried to ignore all the stares and focus on the blackboard, but my glasses kept slipping.

"You there, stop that intolerable fidgeting!" screamed my teacher.

"I'm trying to, Mrs. Brooks," I said. "But my glasses won't stay on because my nose ran away."

"Well, you should have thought of that before class," she said. "Now go home and stay there until you're ready to sit quietly with a nose like everybody else."

Then suddenly, without warning, the most horrible part of the day happened. I sneezed.

"Way to go, No-Nose," called someone from the back of the room.

I walked home in a bad mood. When I got there, my grandfather asked how my day was.

"Lousy."

"No nose, eh?" my grandfather said knowingly. "You know, the same thing happened to me when I was a little boy."

"Really?" I asked, perking up a little.

"Oh, sure. Always sticking my nose in other people's business, I was. Well, one day I stuck it in the neighbor's business and accidentally left it there. I went back the next day to look for it, but it was gone."

"What did you do?"

"I had to go all the way to Nose Island to find it. Years later I lost my hair, but I never found *that* again."

"Nose Island?" I said doubtfully. "There's no such place."

"No such place?" Grandpa almost fell off his chair. "Why, I'll have you know it is one of the most important places in the world, along with Baby Tooth Canyon and Memory Lane. It's where all the unhappy noses go when they're mistreated. In fact, I'll bet your nose is there right now, crying its poor little nostrils out."

The thought of my nose sitting on a strange island, sad and lonely, made me want to cry. But I didn't want to cry and then not be able to blow my nose, so I stopped myself.

"If you want to find your nose again, you need to hitch a ride with the Ship of Lost Things, which sails the Seven Skies scouting for lonely, misplaced objects. It should be by around sunset. Well, good luck," he said, and went back to reading his newspaper.

I ran up to my room to prepare for my voyage. I took only the bare necessities—three candy bars, a change of underwear, and a box of the softest tissues I could find, for when my nose and I were finally reunited. I wanted to take fresh socks, but there was no room. I'd just have to risk offending my feet for a few days.

For hours I sat on the roof, until I lost track of time and the sun turned a tired, rusty red and settled into the distance. Finally, just as night was approaching, I saw a great wooden ship on the horizon. I hoisted a flag up the antenna and waited. Sure enough, the boat turned and floated toward me, bouncing on the bumpy clouds.

Pulling up beside the house, the captain dropped anchor and called down, "Ahoy, matey! Be ye lost?"

"I need to get to Nose Island," I called back.

He dropped a rope ladder down to me. "Shimmy up the line and we'll be off."

I climbed into the boat, and we set sail. The ship was filled to the brim with that night's cargo. In one corner was a whole pile of patience. In another was a big mound of marbles. There was even a huge crate full of baby teeth.

The captain was a little barnacle of a man, with a face that peeked out from his beard like a hermit crab.

"Hey," I said, "I thought the Tooth Fairy took everyone's baby teeth."

"Aren't you a little old to be believing in the Tooth Fairy?" he said. Then he looked carefully at me. "Great dolphin ears! Ye've no nose on yer face, lad!"

I told him my sad story.

"Arrr," said the captain. "Ye should never take yer nose for granted, lad. Two score years did I have me nose, and never a thought did I give it. Then, on one fateful day, I did lose me poor nose—to the White Whale!"

It was then that I noticed the captain's nose was made of wood. "I'll bet a wooden nose isn't so bad," I said. "At least you have one."

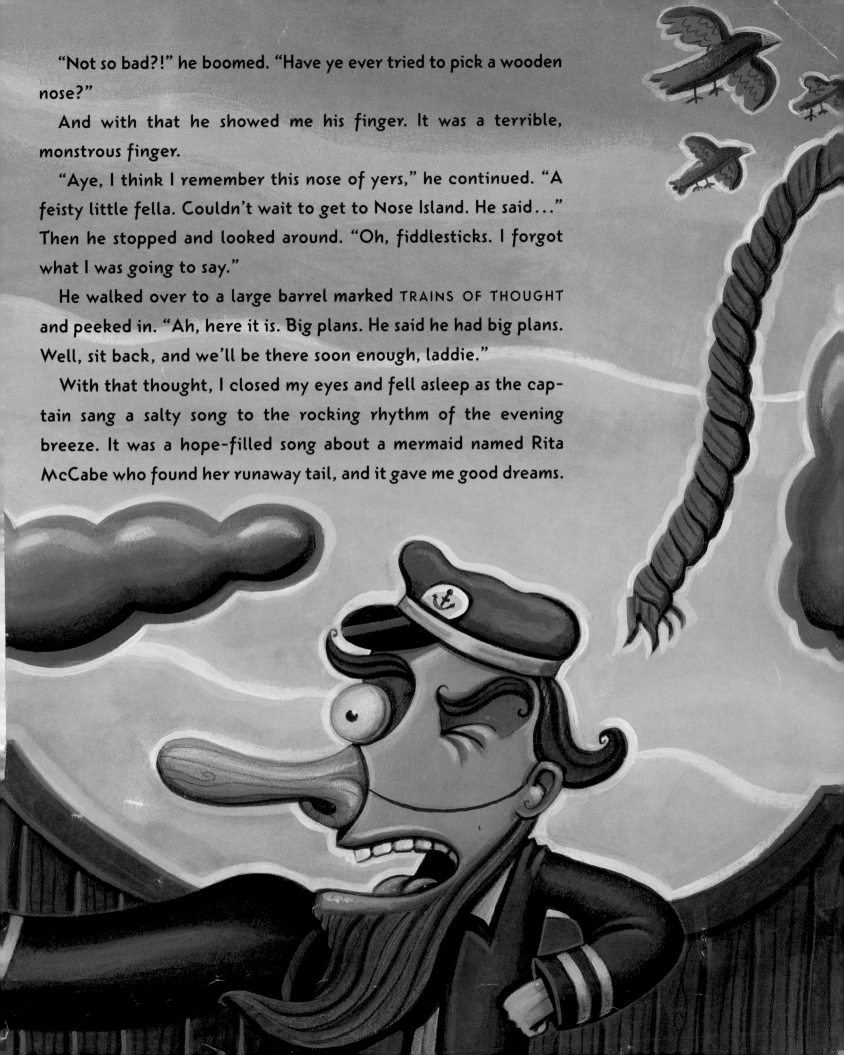

"Not so bad?!" he boomed. "Have ye ever tried to pick a wooden nose?"

And with that he showed me his finger. It was a terrible, monstrous finger.

"Aye, I think I remember this nose of yers," he continued. "A feisty little fella. Couldn't wait to get to Nose Island. He said..." Then he stopped and looked around. "Oh, fiddlesticks. I forgot what I was going to say."

He walked over to a large barrel marked TRAINS OF THOUGHT and peeked in. "Ah, here it is. Big plans. He said he had big plans. Well, sit back, and we'll be there soon enough, laddie."

With that thought, I closed my eyes and fell asleep as the captain sang a salty song to the rocking rhythm of the evening breeze. It was a hope-filled song about a mermaid named Rita McCabe who found her runaway tail, and it gave me good dreams.

When I woke up, the ship had already landed on Nose Island and departed again, leaving me sleeping peacefully on the sunny beach. The captain had left me a message.

ARRR... GOODLUCK

I didn't know what to expect, so I built a disguise out of whatever I could find. Then I set out to explore the island.

Nose Island was an amazing place. There were noses as far as the eye could see, and even farther than the nose could smell. There was every kind of nose imaginable—cute, freckled button noses and big, honking snouts. Some noses were stuffy and some were snooty. There were even a few dog noses that pranced around on tiny leashes.

I looked all over, but my nose was nowhere to be found. I considered adopting a different one, but then thought better of it. I couldn't leave my poor nose here, all sad and alone.

Suddenly a crowd began to gather nearby. They were excitedly applauding for something. I looked around for what it was and quickly found myself engulfed in the stream of whistling, cheering snouts. The crowd got bigger and bigger until it seemed that every nose on the island was there. What horrible luck! I'd never find my poor little nose in a mob that big. And then I looked up.

Sitting on a throne, high above the cheering crowd, was my nose.

Not only had my nose run away to Nose Island—he had become **king** *of it!*

"Let the feast begin!" announced my nose majestically, and a hundred different items were brought out and placed in front of a large bonfire.

"For an appetizer, let us have something sweet and circus-y," said my nose. And with that, a bushel of bright pink cotton candy was thrown into the fire. As the fumes wafted through the crowd, all the noses sniffed hungrily. Dozens of unusual objects followed—orange peels, pizza slices, rose petals, pine needles, bacon, even apple-cinnamon oatmeal.

"That was delicious," said my nose. "And now, dessert. Bring on the popcorn! With butter, of course." Corn kernels exploded into the air and rained down like confetti, thoroughly satisfying every nose in the crowd.

"Whoa, I'm completely stuffed," said my nose, flaring his nostrils happily. "I couldn't smell another thing."

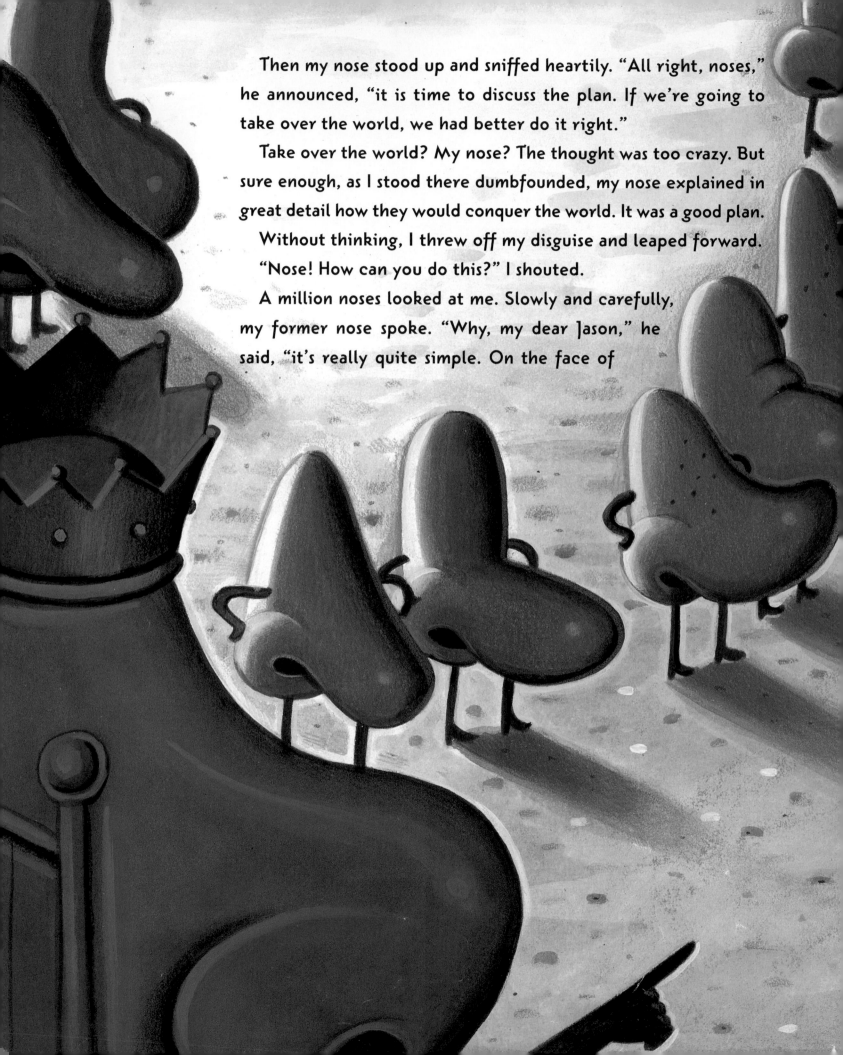

Then my nose stood up and sniffed heartily. "All right, noses," he announced, "it is time to discuss the plan. If we're going to take over the world, we had better do it right."

Take over the world? My nose? The thought was too crazy. But sure enough, as I stood there dumbfounded, my nose explained in great detail how they would conquer the world. It was a good plan.

Without thinking, I threw off my disguise and leaped forward. "Nose! How can you do this?" I shouted.

A million noses looked at me. Slowly and carefully, my former nose spoke. "Why, my dear Jason," he said, "it's really quite simple. On the face of

every man, woman, and child is one of our soldiers, just waiting for the word to rebel. You always thought it was you who carried *us* around. Untrue. It is *we* who have been leading *you!*"

"But I traveled all the way here to bring you back. I even brought tissues—the super-soft kind. You've *got* to come with me," I pleaded.

"Silence, Former Face!" boomed my nose. "Why would I want to leave here? I have everything I want—food, friends, a house on the beach, plus a wife and two little schnozzes. Most important, I have freedom! Now we shall begin the War of the Noses with its first prisoner—you! Seize him!"

As the noses closed in on me, I did the only thing I could think of. I quickly tore off my socks and threw them into the bonfire. I'm embarrassed to say they exploded in a foul cloud of sweaty stink, horrifying every nose on the island.

"Uck!" screamed my former nose. "I thought I'd never have to smell those socks again! They're disgusting!"

I felt bad about making anyone, especially a nose king, smell my

socks. But it was my only escape. I ran as fast as I could, a million angry noses nipping at my heels. I tried to hide, but every time I ducked behind a tree or a rock, a flying toucan beak would swoop down and tell all the noses where I was. A particularly fast one closed in on me. I tossed one of my candy bars on the ground to throw him off my scent. It worked. He stopped to smell the nougat.

Soon the noses began to tire. I could hear them breathing heavily as they struggled to keep up with me. I turned around and saw that every nose had given up the chase. Every nose except one. I wished that I'd had a fatter, more out-of-shape nose.

Just then, in the far, far distance, I saw the Ship of Lost Things sailing past. My only hope was to get close enough so the captain would see me. I ran as fast as I could toward the highest peak on the island.

My nose followed me as I climbed, up and up until we both stood on the mouth of the angry mountain. The captain saw me, but he was still too far away to do anything. I braced myself for my nose's attack.

But my nose just stood there and looked at me sadly.

"I never wanted it to come to this," he said. "We had some good times together, didn't we?"

"Remember that apricot pie Mom made?" I asked.

"Do I!" he said, licking his nostrils. "That smelled amazing. And remember that time you accidentally burned some chocolate-chip cookies? Wasn't that delicious?"

"The best, Montague," I agreed.

"You used my *name*," he said softly. A tear slid down him, and I handed him the soft tissues I'd brought.

"Wow, these *are* soft," he said.

Just then the captain pulled up right above the volcano and shouted down, "Quick, laddie! Climb aboard!"

"You'd better go," said my nose.

"What? You mean you're not coming?"

"Not right now. I've got some things to do first. You'll be fine," he assured me. "Just keep a stiff upper lip."

"From now on," I said, "I intend to keep *all* my body parts." I grabbed hold of the ladder, and the Ship of Lost Things sailed off. In the growing distance, I heard my nose call a farewell.

We sailed directly home, with only a quick stopover at Lost Hair Island, where I got a present for my grandfather. But that's a different story.

I don't know who told you I got my nose back. I hope no one did, because it's not true. I wish I could tell you that my nose eventually came back and we lived happily for years and years and smelled lots of great things together, like flowers and wet dog.

But I can't.

I went to school the next morning sad and scared. I had traveled all the way to Nose Island, and my nose hadn't come home with me. I thought I'd never fit in again.

Until I walked into class. Every single person in the school was completely noseless. Even Mrs. Brooks. My nose, Montague, had convinced all the noses in the world to join him on Nose Island.

He did keep his promise to send me a postcard....